LITTLE MISS VALENTINE

originated by Roger Hargreaves

Written and illustrated by Adam Hargreaves

MR. MEN   **LITTLE MISS**
MR. MEN™ LITTLE MISS™
Copyright © 2019 THOIP
(a SANRIO Company).
All rights reserved.
Used Under License.

GROSSET & DUNLAP
An Imprint of Penguin Random House LLC, New York

Little Miss Valentine™ and © 2019 THOIP (a SANRIO Company). All rights reserved.
Published by Grosset & Dunlap, an imprint of Penguin Random House LLC, New York.
GROSSET & DUNLAP is a trademark of Penguin Random House LLC.
Manufactured in China.

Visit us online at www.penguinrandomhouse.com.

www.mrmen.com

ISBN 9781524793609   10 9 8 7 6 5 4 3 2 1

Little Miss Valentine had one day a year when she was terrifically busy.

Just like Santa Claus on Christmas Day.

Her busy day was filled with deliveries, but she did not deliver presents like Santa does. She delivered valentine cards.

She lived in a heart-shaped house called Cupid Cottage, in Heartland.

On her one very busy day a year, Little Miss Valentine left her cozy cottage to travel around the world and deliver her valentine cards.

You know that Santa Claus has a flying sleigh, pulled by his reindeer.

But what you might not know is that Little Miss Valentine has a hot-air balloon.

A heart-shaped hot-air balloon.

A heart-shaped hot-air balloon pulled by a flock of flamingos!

Little Miss Valentine made all of her deliveries in secret,
in the middle of the night, on the eve of Valentine's Day.

And she had so many cards to deliver!

As she floated over each house, she checked the address,
and then released each envelope, a magic valentine envelope,
which fluttered down on paper wings and into each mailbox.

Everyone loved to receive their valentine card.

Little Miss Chatterbox's card made her chatter with excitement.

Mr. Bump's card made him trip over in delight.

Little Miss Giggle's card made her giggle with glee.

And Little Miss Shy's card made her . . .

. . . blush!

From her rosy cheeks to the very tips of her toes.

Little Miss Valentine's cards were made to match each of her friends.

Little Miss Splendid's card was large and extravagant.

Mr. Mean's card was very small and plain.

Little Miss Scary's card jumped out from the page when she opened it.

So, once a year, Little Miss Valentine was able to deliver a little bit of joy into the lives of each of her friends.

Little Miss Valentine had the best job in the world.

Except for this year.

Because this year was the windiest Valentine's Eve that she had ever seen.

As a howling gale blew leaves around her house, Little Miss Valentine imagined how the wind would blow her cards all over the place when she tried to deliver them.

It would be chaos!

What if the wrong card went into the wrong mailbox?

What if Little Miss Splendid received the card meant for Mr. Mean?

Little Miss Splendid would not be very happy.

And neither would Mr. Mean.

What if Mr. Messy's very messy card went into Little Miss Neat's mailbox?

She would not be very happy.

And what if Mr. Quiet got the card intended for Mr. Noisy?

Little Miss Valentine did not know what to do.

But then she had an idea.

She called her cousin, Little Miss Hug.

Little Miss Hug has very remarkable arms.

Remarkable arms that can hug anybody, whatever their size, because her arms can stretch.

They can stretch all the way up to the clouds to hug Mr. Tall, or they can stretch just a little to go all the way around Mr. Skinny.

But Little Miss Valentine had another use in mind for those remarkable arms.

Little Miss Hug and Little Miss Valentine set off in the hot-air balloon.

The wind blew them along at a terrific speed, and to keep the balloon under control, the flamingos had to flap their wings with all their might.

When they reached the first house, Little Miss Valentine checked the address on the envelope and handed the card to Little Miss Hug.

Little Miss Hug then stretched out one of her extraordinarily stretchy arms and slipped the envelope into the mailbox.

The correct mailbox!

All night long, the two of them delivered all the valentine cards, and in the morning everyone found the right card in their mailbox.

But there was still one card left to deliver, and it was for Little Miss Hug.

It was a perfectly huggable card. And she loved it.

Little Miss Hug was happily hugging her card when she realized that Little Miss Valentine did not have a card.

And there were no cards left in the sack, so she gave Little Miss Valentine the best valentine she could think of . . .

. . . a hug!

It was an extra-special Valentine's Day.